10 Minute Tales

THE WIND MACHINE

Read aloud
Read aloud to your child.

Read alone
Support your child as they read alone.

Read along
Read along with your child.

Read aloud   Read along

Postman Pat has arrived at the mail centre to pick up a special delivery – a wind machine.

"Ted Glen is holding a lesson for Greendale School at his mill," said Ben. "The mill has a water wheel that makes electricity. Ted wants to show the class how the wind machine can power up the mill, too."

"Well, it's a perfect day for it!" said Postman Pat.

Outside the wind was blowing so hard, leaves were whizzing through the air.

Read alone

Postman Pat has a wind machine to deliver.
The machine will power up Ted's mill.

Read aloud   **Read along**

Postman Pat and Ben climbed up to the roof of the mail centre to get the helicopter ready.

But when they reached the top, the wind swept Postman Pat's hat from his head!

"Woah!" Postman Pat cried out, jumping up after his hat.

"Oh dear!" said Ben. "It's far too windy to take the helicopter out. We're going to have to think of something else, Pat."

It is too windy to use the helicopter to deliver the wind machine.

Meanwhile, Lauren's class had just arrived at Ted Glen's mill. They were all playing with toy windmills.

"Ted's machine will whizz around and around, just like these little windmills," said Lauren.

"Cool!" said Julian, spinning the blades around. "When can we see the real machine?"

"Pat should be here any minute," replied Ted. "Then all will be revealed!"

Lauren's class arrive at Ted's mill. They have come to see the wind machine.

Read aloud   Read along

Back at the mail centre, Postman Pat was testing out a new plan.

He had lifted the wind machine onto the fork-lift truck and was trying to get it inside the van. But the fork-lift truck was wobbling about in the wind.

"This way, Pat! Left a bit, right a bit," said Ben.

Finally, the wind machine was safely in the van. Postman Pat and Jess hopped into the front seat and set off for Ted's mill.

Postman Pat puts the wind machine into his van. He sets off for Ted's mill.

Read aloud   Read along

But Postman Pat had only made it to the town square when something flew onto his windscreen.

"What was that?" Postman Pat cried, pressing down hard on the brakes.

The wind had blown Michael Lam's magazines all over Postman Pat's van!

Read alone

Magazines fly onto Postman Pat's van!
He has to stop in the square.

Read aloud   Read along

"Sorry, Pat!" said Michael, chasing after the magazines. "The wind just picked them up and blew them away."

"Don't worry, Michael," said Postman Pat, hopping out of his van. "This wind is dangerous today!"

Postman Pat quickly helped Michael catch the rest of his magazines, then he set off again on his delivery.

Postman Pat helps pick up the magazines.
Then he sets back off on his delivery.

Read aloud Read along

Over at the mill, it was starting to get dark and the wind was causing even more trouble. A branch had got stuck in the water wheel. The wheel stopped turning.

All the lights around the mill fizzed and everything went black.

"Don't worry, children!" said Lauren. "Ted knows how to get the lights working. Right, Ted?"

"Without the wheel, we have no electricity," said Ted. "Until Pat arrives with the wind machine, we're stuck."

Read alone

At Ted's mill, a branch stops the water wheel turning. All the lights go out!

Read aloud   Read along

Postman Pat was driving his van as fast as possible along the country lanes. But at Alf's farm, he had to stop suddenly. A tree had fallen down and the road was blocked.

"There must be another way," said Postman Pat.

Then he noticed a dirt track running through Alf Thompson's field.

"Got it!" said Postman Pat. "Hold on tight, Jess. This is going to be a bumpy ride!"

Read alone

Postman Pat is stuck on the road.
But he finds a shortcut to the mill.

Read aloud   Read along

Postman Pat hadn't gone very far when he heard a strange sound. Baaaa! Baaaa!

It was Rosie – one of Alf's sheep.

"What are you doing out here?" said Postman Pat, "Come on, let's take you home."

When Postman Pat pulled up at the sheep pen, Alf was very happy to see Rosie.

"I've been looking for her all over!" said Alf. "It's not a nice night to be outside, is it, Rosie?"

Rosie the sheep has escaped.
Postman Pat takes her back to Alf's farm.

Read aloud   Read along

Suddenly, a huge gust of wind blew through the pen. The wooden gate came loose. It whizzed through the air and crashed into Postman Pat's van!

The engine made a loud spluttering noise and then went silent.

Postman Pat opened up the bonnet.

"Oh dear, the engine is broken," said Postman Pat. "The children will be waiting for my delivery. Now what am I going to do?"

Read alone

Alf's gate crashes into Postman Pat's van. The engine is broken!

Read aloud   Read along

Alf peered inside the back of the van and saw the wind machine.

"Ah, it's a real shame the kids won't see this," Alf said. "On a day like today, that machine would be spinning like crazy!"

Postman Pat thought for a second.

"Alf ... you may have just cracked it. The wind machine can power the van! When the wind blows, the blades will turn and push the van forward."

Postman Pat has an idea.
The wind machine can power the van.

Sure enough, when the wind started to blow, the wind machine swirled into action and the van moved forward.

"It works!" cried Postman Pat, as the van started to gather speed.

Postman Pat and Jess quickly jumped into the moving van.

"'Bye, Alf!" Postman Pat shouted out of the window. "One windy delivery, back on track!"

Read alone

The wind machine moves the van forward.
Postman Pat is back on his delivery!

Read aloud   Read along

At Ted's mill, the children were all huddled around a lantern in the shed.

"Miss, it's spooky in here," Sarah said. "Are there monsters outside?"

"No, Sarah," Lauren replied. "There's nothing outside ..."

Suddenly, there was a loud bang on the door.

"Then what was that?" gasped Julian.

The children are scared of the dark.
They hear a loud bang on the mill door!

Read alone

Read aloud   Read along

"Hello, everyone!" came a voice through the door. It was Postman Pat!

"You made it!" said Ted, as everyone cheered. "Now let's get these lights back on."

Bill and Sarah helped Ted hook the wind machine up to the light supply. Everybody watched the machine.

Nothing happened.

The wind had stopped!